THE MISSING ANTIMATTER

GAURAV SINGH PATEL

ISBN 979-888569313-4

Contents

Preface

As we know that when the Universe was starting, Matter and Anti-Matter were made in equal quantity, then in today's time we get to see only Matter all around us, where did that Anti-Matter go. This question remains a mystery till date. So in this book, I have first collected the definitions of Antimatter from various mediums and have written them first and after that I have presented the answer to what was called Anti Matter on the basis of my research, which is the last topic of this book.

GAURAV SINGH PATEL
(Researcher of Astronomy Physics)

Preface

As we know that when the Universe was [illegible] Matter and Anti Matter were made in equal quantities then in today's time we get [illegible] only Matter all around us [illegible] Anti-Matter [illegible] question remains [illegible] collected the definition [illegible] from [illegible] have written them first [illegible] I have presented [illegible] to [illegible] Anti Matter [illegible] the basis of [illegible] this book.

[illegible]

CHAPTER ONE

According To Britannica

antimatter, substance composed of subatomic particles that have the mass, electric charge, and magnetic moment of the electrons, protons, and neutrons of ordinary matter but for which the electric charge and magnetic moment are opposite in sign. The antimatter particles corresponding to electrons, protons, and neutrons are called positrons (e+), antiprotons (p), and antineutrons (n); collectively they are referred to as antiparticles. The electrical properties of antimatter being opposite to those of ordinary matter, the positron has a positive charge and the antiproton a negative charge; the antineutron, though electrically neutral, has a magnetic moment opposite in sign to that of the neutron. Matter and antimatter cannot coexist at close range for more than a small fraction of a second because they collide with and annihilate each other, releasing large quantities of energy in the form of gamma rays or elementary particles.

The concept of antimatter first arose in theoretical analysis of the duality between positive and negative charge. The work of P.A.M. Dirac on the energy states of the electron implied the existence of a particle identical in every respect but one—that is, with positive instead of negative charge. Such a particle, called the positron, is not to be found in ordinary stable matter. However, it was discovered in 1932 among particles produced in the interactions of cosmic rays in matter and thus provided experimental confirmation of Dirac's theory.

The life expectancy or duration of the positron in ordinary matter is very short. Unless the positron is moving extremely fast, it will be drawn close to an ordinary electron by the attraction between opposite charges. A collision between the positron and the electron results in their simultaneous disappearance, their masses (m) being converted into energy (E) in accordance with the Einstein mass-energy relation E = mc2, where c is the velocity of light. This process is called annihilation, and the resultant energy is emitted in the form of gamma rays (γ), high-energy quanta of electromagnetic radiation. The inverse reaction γ → e+ + e− can also proceed under appropriate conditions, and the process is called electron-positron creation, or pair production.

The Dirac theory predicts that an electron and a positron, because of Coulomb attraction of their opposite charges, will combine to form an intermediate bound state, just as an electron and a proton combine to form a hydrogen atom. The e+e− bound system is called positronium. The annihilation of positronium into gamma rays has been observed. Its measured lifetime depends on the orientation of the two particles and is on the order of 10−10–10−7 second, in agreement with that computed from Dirac's theory.

The Dirac wave equation also describes the behaviour of both protons and neutrons and thus predicts the existence of their antiparticles. Antiprotons can be produced by bombarding protons with protons. If enough energy is available—that is, if the incident proton has a kinetic energy of at least 5.6 gigaelectron volts (GeV; 109 eV)—extra particles of proton mass will appear according to the formula E = mc2. Such energies became available in the 1950s at the Bevatron particle accelerator at Berkeley, California. In 1955 a team of physicists led by Owen Chamberlain and Emilio Segrè observed that antiprotons are produced by high-energy collisions. Antineutrons also were discovered at the Bevatron by observing their annihilation in matter with a consequent release of high-energy electromagnetic radiation.

By the time the antiproton was discovered, a host of new subatomic particles had also been discovered; all these particles are now known to have corresponding antiparticles. Thus, there are positive and negative muons, positive and negative pi-mesons, and the K-meson and the anti-K-meson, plus a long list of baryons and antibaryons. Most of these newly discovered particles have too short a lifetime to be able to combine with electrons. The exception is the positive muon, which, together with an electron, has been observed to form a muonium atom.

In 1995 physicists at the European Organization for Nuclear Research (CERN) in Geneva created the first antiatom, the antimatter counterpart of an ordinary atom—in this case, antihydrogen, the simplest antiatom, consisting of a positron in orbit around an antiproton nucleus. They did so by firing antiprotons through a xenon-gas jet. In the strong electric fields surrounding the xenon nuclei, some antiprotons created pairs of electrons and positrons; a few of the positrons thus produced then combined with the antiprotons to form antihydrogen. Each antiatom survived for only about 40-billionths of a second before it came into contact with ordinary matter and was annihilated. CERN has since produced larger amounts of antihydrogen that can last 1,000 seconds. A comparison of the spectrum of the antihydrogen atom with the well-studied spectrum of hydrogen could reveal small differences between matter and antimatter, which would have important implications for theories of how matter formed in the early universe.

In 2010 physicists using the Relativistic Heavy Ion Collider at Brookhaven National Laboratory in Upton, New York, used a billion collisions between gold ions to create 18 instances of the heaviest antiatom, the nucleus of antihelium-4, which consists of two antiprotons and two antineutrons. Since antihelium-4 is produced so rarely in nuclear collisions, its detection in space by an instrument such as the Alpha Magnetic Spectrometer on the International Space Station would imply the existence of large amounts of antimatter in the universe.

Although positrons are readily created in the collisions of cosmic rays, there is no evidence for the existence of large amounts of antimatter in the universe. The Milky Way Galaxy appears to consist entirely of matter, as there are no indications for regions where matter and antimatter meet and annihilate to produce characteristic gamma rays. The implication that matter completely dominates antimatter in the universe appears to be in contradiction to Dirac's theory, which, supported by experiment, shows that particles and antiparticles are always created in equal numbers from energy. (See electron-positron pair production.) The energetic conditions of the early universe should have created equal numbers of particles and antiparticles; mutual annihilation of particle-antiparticle pairs, however, would have left nothing but energy. In the universe today, photons (energy) outnumber protons (matter) by a factor of one billion. This suggests that most of the particles created in the early universe were indeed annihilated by antiparticles, while one in a billion particles had no matching antiparticle and so survived to form the matter observed today in stars and galaxies. The tiny imbalance between particles and antiparticles in the early universe is referred to as matter-antimatter asymmetry, and its cause remains a major unsolved puzzle for cosmology and particle physics. One possible explanation is that it involves a phenomenon known as CP violation, which gives rise to a small but significant difference in the behaviour of particles called K-mesons and their antiparticles. This explanation for the asymmetry gained credence in 2010, when CP violation was seen in the decay of B-mesons, particles that are heavier than K-mesons and thus able to account for more of the asymmetry.

CHAPTER TWO

Page Of Symmetry Magazine

Ten things you might not know about antimatter

Antimatter is the stuff of science fiction. In the book and film Angels and Demons, Professor Langdon tries to save Vatican City from an antimatter bomb. Star Trek's starship Enterprise uses matter-antimatter annihilation propulsion for faster-than-light travel.

But antimatter is also the stuff of reality. Antimatter particles are almost identical to their matter counterparts except that they carry the opposite charge and spin. When antimatter meets matter, they immediately annihilate into energy.

While antimatter bombs and antimatter-powered spaceships are far-fetched, there are still many facts about antimatter that will tickle your brain cells.

Illustrations by Sandbox Studio, Chicago with Ana Kova

1. Antimatter should have annihilated all of the matter in the universe after the big bang.

According to theory, the big bang should have created matter and antimatter in equal amounts. When matter and antimatter meet, they annihilate, leaving nothing but energy behind. So in principle, none of us should exist.

But we do. And as far as physicists can tell, it's only because, in the end, there was one extra matter particle for every billion matter-antimatter pairs. Physicists are hard at work trying to explain this asymmetry.

Illustrations by Sandbox Studio, Chicago with Ana Kova

2. Antimatter is closer to you than you think.

Small amounts of antimatter constantly rain down on the Earth in the form of cosmic rays, energetic particles from space. These antimatter particles reach our atmosphere at a rate ranging from less than one per square meter to more than 100 per square meter. Scientists have also seen evidence of antimatter production above thunderstorms.

But other antimatter sources are even closer to home. For example, bananas produce antimatter, releasing one positron—the antimatter equivalent of an electron—about every 75 minutes. This occurs because bananas contain a small amount of potassium-40, a naturally occurring isotope of potassium. As potassium-40 decays, it occasionally spits out a positron in the process.

Our bodies also contain potassium-40, which means positrons are being emitted from you, too. Antimatter annihilates immediately on contact with matter, so these antimatter particles are very short-lived.

Illustrations by Sandbox Studio, Chicago with Ana Kova

3. Humans have created only a tiny amount of antimatter.

Antimatter-matter annihilations have the potential to release a huge amount of energy. A gram of antimatter could produce an explosion the size of a nuclear bomb. However, humans have produced only a minuscule amount of antimatter.

All of the antiprotons created at Fermilab's Tevatron particle accelerator add up to only 15 nanograms. Those made at CERN amount to about 1 nanogram. At DESY in Germany, approximately 2 nanograms of positrons have been produced to date.

If all the antimatter ever made by humans were annihilated at once, the energy produced wouldn't even be enough to boil a cup of tea.

The problem lies in the efficiency and cost of antimatter production and storage. Making 1 gram of antimatter would require approximately 25 million billion kilowatt-hours of energy and cost over a million billion dollars.

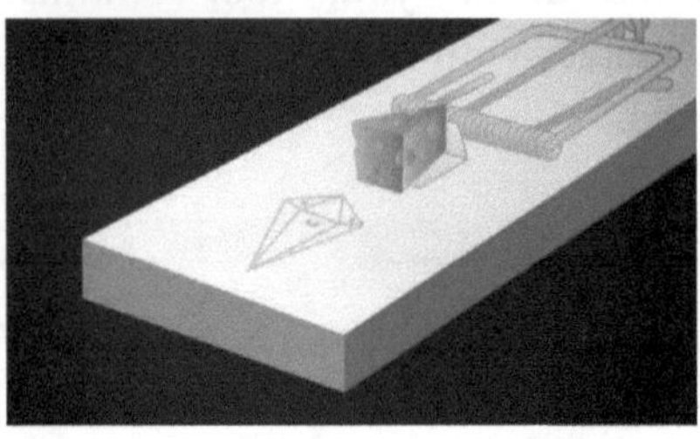

Illustrations by Sandbox Studio, Chicago with Ana Kova

4. There is such a thing as an antimatter trap.

To study antimatter, you need to prevent it from annihilating with matter. Scientists have created ways to do just that.

Charged antimatter particles such as positrons and antiprotons can be held in devices called Penning traps. These are comparable to tiny accelerators. Inside, particles spiral around as the magnetic and electric fields keep them from colliding with the walls of the trap.

But Penning traps won't work on neutral particles such as antihydrogen. Because they have no charge, these particles cannot be confined by electric fields. Instead, they are held in Ioffe traps, which work by creating a region of space where the magnetic field gets larger in all directions. The particle gets stuck in the area with the weakest magnetic field, much like a marble rolling around the bottom of a bowl.

Earth's magnetic field can also act as a sort of antimatter trap. Antiprotons have been found in zones around the Earth called Van Allen radiation belts.

Illustrations by Sandbox Studio, Chicago with Ana Kova

5. Antimatter might fall up.

Antimatter and matter particles have the same mass but differ in properties such as electric charge and spin. The Standard Model predicts that gravity should have the same effect on matter and antimatter; however, this has yet to be seen. Experiments such as AEGIS, ALPHA and GBAR are hard at work trying to find out.

Observing gravity's effect on antimatter is not quite as easy as watching an apple fall from a tree. These experiments need to hold antimatter in a trap or slow it down by cooling it to temperatures just above absolute zero. And because gravity is the weakest of the fundamental forces, physicists must use neutral antimatter particles in these experiments to prevent interference by the more powerful electrical force.

Illustrations by Sandbox Studio, Chicago with Ana Kova

6. Antimatter is studied in particle decelerators.

You've heard of particle accelerators, but did you know there were also particle decelerators? CERN houses a machine called the Antiproton Decelerator, a storage ring that can capture and slow antiprotons to study their properties and behavior.

In circular particle accelerators like the Large Hadron Collider, particles get a kick of energy each time they complete a rotation. Decelerators work in reverse; instead of an energy boost, particles get a kick backward to slow their speeds.

Illustrations by Sandbox Studio, Chicago with Ana Kova

7. Neutrinos might be their own antiparticles.

A matter particle and its antimatter partner carry opposite charges, making them easy to distinguish. Neutrinos, nearly massless particles that rarely interact with matter, have no charge. Scientists believe that they may be Majorana particles, a hypothetical class of particles that are their own antiparticles.

Projects such as the Majorana Demonstrator and EXO-200 are aimed at determining whether neutrinos are Majorana particles by looking for a behavior called neutrinoless double-beta decay.

Some radioactive nuclei simultaneously decay, releasing two electrons and two neutrinos. If neutrinos were their own antiparticles, they would annihilate each other in the aftermath of the double decay, and scientists would observe only electrons.

Finding Majorana neutrinos could help explain why antimatter-matter asymmetry exists. Physicists hypothesize that Majorana neutrinos can either be heavy or light. The light ones exist today, and the heavy ones would have only existed right after the big bang. These heavy Majorana neutrinos would have decayed asymmetrically, leading to the tiny matter excess that allowed our universe to exist.

Illustrations by Sandbox Studio, Chicago with Ana Kova

8. Antimatter is used in medicine.

PET (positron emission tomography) uses positrons to produce high-resolution images of the body. Positron-emitting radioactive isotopes (like the ones found in bananas) are attached to chemical substances such as glucose that are used naturally by the body. These are injected into the bloodstream, where they are naturally broken down, releasing positrons that meet electrons in the body and annihilate. The annihilations produce gamma rays that are used to construct images.

Scientists on CERN's ACE project have studied antimatter as a potential candidate for cancer therapy. Physicians have already discovered that they can target tumors with beams of particles that will release their energy only after safely passing through healthy tissue. Using antiprotons adds an extra burst of energy. The technique was found to be effective in hamster cells, but researchers have yet to conduct studies in human cells.

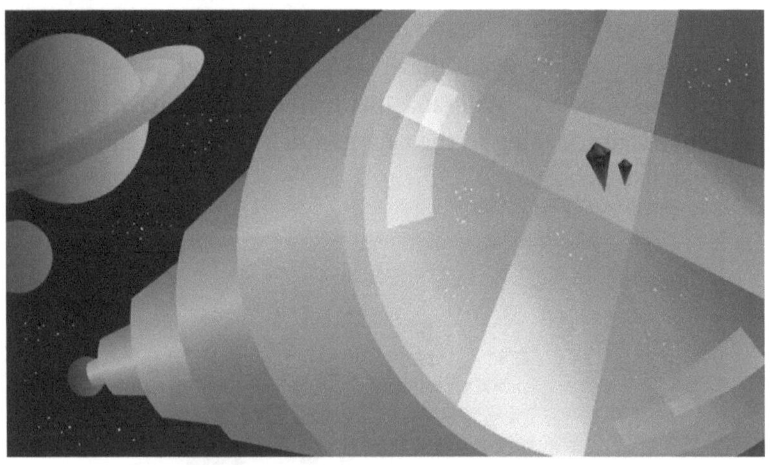

Illustrations by Sandbox Studio, Chicago with Ana Kova

9. The antimatter that should have prevented us from existing might still be lurking in space.

One way that scientists are trying to solve the antimatter-matter asymmetry problem is by looking for antimatter left over from the big bang.

The Alpha Magnetic Spectrometer is a particle detector that sits atop the International Space Station searching for these particles. AMS contains magnetic fields that bend the path of cosmic particles to separate matter from antimatter. Its detectors assess and identify the particles as they pass through.

Cosmic ray collisions routinely produce positrons and antiprotons, but the probability of creating an antihelium atom is extremely low because of the huge amount of energy it would require. This means the observation of even a single antihelium nucleus would be strong evidence for the existence a large amount of antimatter somewhere else in the universe.

Illustrations by Sandbox Studio, Chicago with Ana Kova

10. People are actually studying how to fuel spacecraft with antimatter.

Just a handful of antimatter can produce a huge amount of power, making it a popular fuel for futuristic vehicles in science fiction.

Antimatter rocket propulsion is hypothetically possible; the major limitation is gathering enough antimatter to make it happen.

There is currently no technology available to mass-produce or collect antimatter in the volume needed for this application. However, a small number of researchers have conducted simulation studies on propulsion and storage. These include Ronan Keane and Wei-Ming Zhang, who did their work at Western Reserve Academy and Kent State University, respectively, and Marc Weber and his colleagues at Washington State University. One day, if we can figure out a way to create or collect large amounts of antimatter, their studies might help antimatter-propelled interstellar travel become a reality.

CHAPTER THREE

Statement Of Cern

Antimatter detectives

The antimatter is missing – not from CERN, but from the Universe! At least that is what we can deduce so far from careful examination of the evidence. For each basic particle of matter, there exists an antiparticle with the same mass, but the opposite electric charge. The negatively charged electron, for example, has a positively charged antiparticle called the positron. When a particle and its antiparticle come together, they both disappear, quite literally in a flash, as the annihilation process transforms their mass into energy.

The evidence spoke for itself

The 'case file' of antimatter was opened in 1928 by physicist Paul Dirac. He developed a theory that combined quantum mechanics and Einstein's special relativity to provide a more complete description of electron interactions. The basic equation he derived turned out to have two solutions, one for the electron and one that seemed to describe something with positive charge (in fact, it was the positron). Then in 1932 the evidence was found to prove these ideas correct, when the positron was discovered occurring naturally in cosmic rays.

For the past 50 years and more, laboratories like CERN have routinely produced antiparticles, and in 1995 CERN became the first laboratory to create anti-atoms artificially. But no one has ever produced antimatter without also obtaining the corresponding matter particles. The scenario should have been the same during the birth of the Universe, when equal amounts of matter and antimatter would have been produced in the Big Bang.

"Just one more thing..."

So if matter and antimatter annihilate, and we and everything else are made of matter, why do we still exist? This mystery arises because we find ourselves living in a Universe made exclusively of matter. Didn't matter and antimatter completely annihilate at the time of the Big Bang? Perhaps this antimatter still exists somewhere else? Otherwise where did it go and what happened to it in the first place?

Such questions have led to speculative theories, from a break in the rules to the existence of an entire anti-Universe somewhere else! The way to solve the baffling disappearance of antimatter, and to learn more about this substance in general, is by studying both particles and antiparticles to find and decipher the subtle clues.

CHAPTER FOUR

Term Of Scientific American

R. Michael Barnett of the Lawrence Berkeley National Laboratory and Helen Quinn of the Stanford Linear Accelerator Center offer this answer, portions of which are paraphrased from their book The Charm of Strange Quarks:

In 1930 Paul Dirac formulated a quantum theory for the motion of electrons in electric and magnetic fields, the first theory that correctly included Einstein's theory of special relativity in this context. This theory led to a surprising predictionthe equations that described the electron also described, and in fact required, the existence of another type of particle with exactly the same mass as the electron but with positive instead of negative electric charge. This particle, which is called the positron, is the antiparticle of the electron, and it was the first example of antimatter.

Its discovery in experiments soon confirmed the remarkable prediction of antimatter in Dirac's theory. A cloud chamber picture taken by Carl D. Anderson in 1931 showed a particle entering from below and passing through a lead plate. The direction of the curvature of the path, caused by a magnetic field, indicated that the particle was a positively charged one but with the same mass and other characteristics as an electron. Experiments today routinely produce large numbers of positrons.

Dirac's prediction applies not only to the electron but to all the fundamental constituents of matter (particles). Each type of particle must have a corresponding antiparticle type. The mass of any antiparticle is identical to that of the particle. All the rest of its properties are also closely related but with the signs of all charges reversed. For example, a proton has a positive electric charge, but an antiproton has a negative electric charge. The existence of antimatter partners for all matter particles is now a well-verified phenomenon, with both partners for hundreds of such pairings observed.

New discoveries lead to new language. In coining the term "antimatter," physicists in fact redefined the meaning of the word "matter." Until that time, "matter" meant anything with substance; even today school textbooks give this definition: "matter takes up space and has mass." By adding the concept of antimatter as distinct from matter, physicists narrowed the definition of matter to apply to only certain kinds of particles, including, however, all those found in everyday experience.

Any pair of matching particle and antiparticle can be produced anytime there is sufficient energy available to provide the necessary mass-energy. Similarly, anytime a particle meets its matching antiparticle, the two can annihilate each anotherthat is, they both disappear, leaving their energy transformed into some other form.

There is no intrinsic difference between particles and antiparticles; they appear on essentially the same footing in all particle theories. This means that the laws of physics for antiparticles are almost identical to those for particles; any difference is a tiny effect. But there certainly is a dramatic difference in the numbers of these objects we find in the world around us; all the world is made of matter. Any antimatter we produce in the laboratory soon disappears because it meets up with matching matter particles and annihilates.

Modern theories of particle physics and of the evolution of the universe suggest, or even require, that antimatter and matter were equally common in the earliest stagesso why is antimatter so uncommon today? The observed imbalance between matter and antimatter is a puzzle yet to be explained. Without it, the universe today would certainly be a much less interesting place, because there would be essentially no matter left around; annihilations would have converted everything into electromagnetic radiation by now. So clearly this imbalance is a key property of the world we know. Attempts to explain it are an active area of research today.

In order to answer this question, we need to better understand that tiny part of the laws of physics that differ for matter and antimatter; without such a difference, there would be no way for an imbalance to occur. This distinction is the subject of study in a number of experiments around the world that focus on differences in the decays of particles called B-mesons and their antiparticle partners. These experiments will be done both at electron-positron collider facilities called B factories and at high-energy hadron colliders, because each type of facility offers different capabilities to contribute to the study of this detail of the laws of physics--a detail that is responsible for such an important property of the universe as the fact that there is anything there at all!

Maria Spiropulu is a physics doctoral candidate at Harvard. Her response follows:

Let's start by defining matter. People have asked "what is matter?" for quite a long time. Democritus, the ancient Greek philosopher and mathematician, envisioned structure in the building blocks of everything and he called the basis for this structure an atom; he wrote, "nothing exists except atoms and empty space: everything else is opinion." At the atomic level, the world can be described in terms of the elements, including hydrogen, oxygen, carbon and the like.

As it turns out, though, atoms are not the fundamental constituents of matter. When we zoom closer into matter, by probing at smaller distances, the subatomic world unfolds. The closer we look, the stranger this world, the quantum world, actually behaves. We can not make a direct connection with it: at a small scale, objects do not behave like rods or balls or waves or clouds or anything we have ever directly experienced. But the quantum mechanics of this world does let us describe how atoms form molecules.

It also enables us to depict the "motion" of certain particles inside atoms. Indeed, atoms are made of electrons that whiz around the fixed protons and neutrons in their nuclei, which are made of quarks. These particles all interact with each other by means of "force messenger" particles, such as photons, gluons, W's and Z's. Based on the attributes of these particles, we assign them identification numbers, or quantum numbers. And by means of symmetries and conservation laws involving the quantum numbers of the particles, we can describe their interactions. Examples of such numbers are charge and intrinsic angular momentum, or spin.

If a is any particle and this particle has no attributes other than linear and angular momentum (which include energy and spin), then a is its own anti-particle--one of the constituents of antimatter. For example, the photon is its own anti-particle. If a particle has other attributes (such as an electric charge Q), then the anti-particle has the opposite attributes (or a charge of -Q). The proton and neutron have such attributes. In the case of the proton, its positive charge distinguishes it from the negatively charged anti-proton. The neutron--although electrically neutral--has a magnetic moment opposite that of the anti-neutron. Protons and neutrons have another quantum number called the baryon number, which also has the opposite sign in the corresponding anti-particles.

The operation of changing particles with anti-particles is called Charge conjugation (C). Particles and anti-particles have the exact same mass and equal, but opposite charges and magnetic moments; if they are unstable, they have the same lifetime. This period is called the Charge Conjugation-Parity-Time (CPT) invariance, which establishes the fact that if you interchange particles for anti-particles (C), look in a three dimensional mirror (P) and reverse time (T), you cannot tell the difference between the them. The most stringent tests of CPT to date are measurements of the ratio of the magnetic moments of the electron and positron to two parts in a trillion (R. Van Dyck, Jr. and P. B. Schwinberg, University of Washington,1987) and measurements of charge per mass of the proton and antiproton--found to be 0.999,999,999,91 to 90 parts per trillion (G. Gabrielse, Harvard, 1998).

Antimatter came about as a solution to the fact that the equation describing a free particle in motion (the relativistic relation between energy, momentum and mass) has not only positive energy solutions, but negative ones as well! If this were true, nothing would stop a particle from falling down to infinite negative energy states, emitting an infinite amount of energy in the process--something which does not happen. In 1928, Paul Dirac postulated the existence of positively charged electrons. The result was an equation describing both matter and antimatter in terms of quantum fields. This work was a truly historic triumph, because it was experimentally confirmed and it inaugurated a new way of thinking about particles and fields.

In 1932, Carl Anderson discovered the positron while measuring cosmic rays in a Wilson chamber experiment. In 1955 at the Berkeley Bevatron, Emilio Segre, Owen Chamberlain, Clyde Wiegand and Thomas Ypsilantis discovered the antiproton. And in 1995 at CERN, scientists synthesized anti-hydrogen atoms for the first time.

When a particle and its anti-particle collide, they annihilate into energy, which is carried by "force messenger" particles that can subsequently decay into other particles. For example, when a proton and anti-proton annihilate at high energies, a top-anti-top quark pair can be created!

An intriguing puzzle arises when we consider that the laws of physics treat matter and antimatter almost symmetrically. Why then don't we have encounters with anti-people made of anti-atoms? Why is it that the stars, dust and everything else we observe is made of matter? If the cosmos began with equal amounts of matter and antimatter, where is the antimatter?

Experimentally, the absence of annihilation radiation from the Virgo cluster shows that little antimatter can be found within ~20 Megaparsecs (Mpc), the typical size of galactic clusters. Even so, a rich program of searches for antimatter in cosmic radiation exists. Among others, results form the High-Energy Antimatter Telescope, a balloon cosmic ray experiment, as well as those from 100 hours worth of data from the Alpha Magnetic Spectrometer aboard NASA's Space Shuttle, support the matter dominance in our Universe. Results from NASA's orbiting Compton Gamma Ray Observatory , however, are uncovering what might be clouds and fountains of antimatter in the Galactic Center.

We stated that there is an approximate symmetry between matter and antimatter. The small asymmetry is thought to be at least partly responsible for the fact that matter outlives antimatter in our universe. Recently both the NA48 experiment at CERN and the KTeV experiment at Fermilab have directly measured this asymmetry with enough precision to establish it. And a number of experiments, including the BaBar experiment at the Stanford Linear Accelerator Center and Belle at KEK in Japan, will confront the same question in different particle systems.

Antimatter at lower energies is used in Positron Emission Tomography (see this PET image of the brain). But antimatter has captured public interest mainly as fuel for the fictional starship Enterprise on Star Trek. In fact, NASA is paying attention to antimatter as a possible fuel for interstellar propulsion. At Penn State University, the Antimatter Space Propulsion group is addressing the challenge of using antimatter annihilation as source of energy for propulsion. See you on Mars?

CHAPTER FIVE

The Standard Model

The theories and discoveries of thousands of physicists since the 1930s have resulted in a remarkable insight into the fundamental structure of matter: everything in the universe is found to be made from a few basic building blocks called fundamental particles, governed by four fundamental forces. Our best understanding of how these particles and three of the forces are related to each other is encapsulated in the Standard Model of particle physics. Developed in the early 1970s, it has successfully explained almost all experimental results and precisely predicted a wide variety of phenomena. Over time and through many experiments, the Standard Model has become established as a well-tested physics theory.

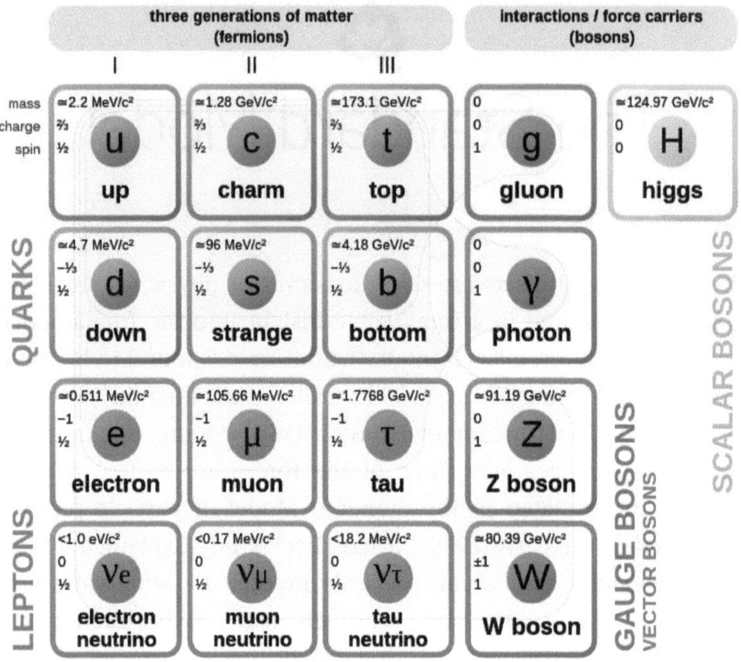

Matter particles

All matter around us is made of elementary particles, the building blocks of matter. These particles occur in two basic types called quarks and leptons. Each group consists of six particles, which are related in pairs, or "generations". The lightest and most stable particles make up the first generation, whereas the heavier and less-stable particles belong to the second and third generations. All stable matter in the universe is made from particles that belong to the first generation; any heavier particles quickly decay to more stable ones. The six quarks are paired in three generations – the "up quark" and the "down quark" form the first generation, followed by the "charm quark" and "strange quark", then the "top quark" and "bottom (or beauty) quark". Quarks also come in three different "colours" and only mix in such ways as to form colourless objects. The six leptons are similarly arranged in three generations – the "electron" and the "electron neutrino", the "muon" and the "muon neutrino", and the "tau" and the "tau neutrino". The electron, the muon and the tau all have an electric charge and a sizeable mass, whereas the neutrinos are electrically neutral and have very little mass.

Forces and carrier particles

There are four fundamental forces at work in the universe: the strong force, the weak force, the electromagnetic force, and the gravitational force. They work over different ranges and have different strengths. Gravity is the weakest but it has an infinite range. The electromagnetic force also has infinite range but it is many times stronger than gravity. The weak and strong forces are effective only over a very short range and dominate only at the level of subatomic particles. Despite its name, the weak force is much stronger than gravity but it is indeed the weakest of the other three. The strong force, as the name suggests, is the strongest of all four fundamental interactions.

Three of the fundamental forces result from the exchange of force-carrier particles, which belong to a broader group called "bosons". Particles of matter transfer discrete amounts of energy by exchanging bosons with each other. Each fundamental force has its own corresponding boson – the strong force is carried by the "gluon", the electromagnetic force is carried by the "photon", and the "W and Z bosons" are responsible for the weak force. Although not yet found, the "graviton" should be the corresponding force-carrying particle of gravity. The Standard Model includes the electromagnetic, strong and weak forces and all their carrier particles, and explains well how these forces act on all of the matter particles. However, the most familiar force in our everyday lives, gravity, is not part of the Standard Model, as fitting gravity comfortably into this framework has proved to be a difficult challenge. The quantum theory used to describe the micro world, and the general theory of relativity used to describe the macro world, are difficult to fit into a single framework. No one has managed to make the two mathematically compatible in the context of the Standard Model. But luckily for particle physics, when it comes to the minuscule scale of particles, the effect of gravity is so weak as to be negligible. Only when matter is in bulk, at the scale of the human body or of the planets for example, does the effect of gravity dominate. So the Standard Model still works well despite its reluctant exclusion of one of the fundamental forces.

So far so good, but...

...it is not time for physicists to call it a day just yet. Even though the Standard Model is currently the best description there is of the subatomic world, it does not explain the complete picture. The theory incorporates only three out of the four fundamental forces, omitting gravity. There are also important questions that it does not answer, such as "What is dark matter?", or "What happened to the antimatter after the big bang?", "Why are there three generations of quarks and leptons with such a different mass scale?" and more. Last but not least is a particle called the Higgs boson, an essential component of the Standard Model.

On 4 July 2012, the ATLAS and CMS experiments at CERN's Large Hadron Collider (LHC) announced they had each observed a new particle in the mass region around 126 GeV. This particle is consistent with the Higgs boson but it will take further work to determine whether or not it is the Higgs boson predicted by the Standard Model. The Higgs boson, as proposed within the Standard Model, is the simplest manifestation of the Brout-Englert-Higgs mechanism. Other types of Higgs bosons are predicted by other theories that go beyond the Standard Model.

On 8 October 2013 the Nobel prize in physics was awarded jointly to François Englert and Peter Higgs “for the theoretical discovery of a mechanism that contributes to our understanding of the origin of mass of subatomic particles, and which recently was confirmed through the discovery of the predicted fundamental particle, by the ATLAS and CMS experiments at CERN’s Large Hadron Collider”.

So although the Standard Model accurately describes the phenomena within its domain, it is still incomplete. Perhaps it is only a part of a bigger picture that includes new physics hidden deep in the subatomic world or in the dark recesses of the universe. New information from experiments at the LHC will help us to find more of these missing pieces.

CHAPTER SIX

The Large Hadron Collider (LHC)

The Large Hadron Collider (LHC) is the world's largest and most powerful particle accelerator. It first started up on 10 September 2008, and remains the latest addition to CERN's accelerator complex. The LHC consists of a 27-kilometre ring of superconducting magnets with a number of accelerating structures to boost the energy of the particles along the way.

Inside the accelerator, two high-energy particle beams travel at close to the speed of light before they are made to collide. The beams travel in opposite directions in separate beam pipes – two tubes kept at ultrahigh vacuum. They are guided around the accelerator ring by a strong magnetic field maintained by superconducting electromagnets. The electromagnets are built from coils of special electric cable that operates in a superconducting state, efficiently conducting electricity without resistance or loss of energy. This requires chilling the magnets to -271.3°C – a temperature colder than outer space. For this reason, much of the accelerator is connected to a distribution system of liquid helium, which cools the magnets, as well as to other supply services.

Large Hadron Collider (LHC)

Thousands of magnets of different varieties and sizes are used to direct the beams around the accelerator. These include 1232 dipole magnets 15 metres in length which bend the beams, and 392 quadrupole magnets, each 5–7 metres long, which focus the beams. Just prior to collision, another type of magnet is used to "squeeze" the particles closer together to increase the chances of collisions. The particles are so tiny that the task of making them collide is akin to firing two needles 10 kilometres apart with such precision that they meet halfway.

All the controls for the accelerator, its services and technical infrastructure are housed under one roof at the CERN Control Centre. From here, the beams inside the LHC are made to collide at four locations around the accelerator ring, corresponding to the positions of four particle detectors – ATLAS, CMS, ALICE and LHCb.

CHAPTER SEVEN

The Conversation

Antimatter was one of the most exciting physics discoveries of the 20th century. Picked up by fiction writers such as Dan Brown, many people think of it as an "out there" theoretical idea – unaware that it is actually being produced every day. What's more, research on antimatter is actually helping us to understand how the universe works.

Antimatter is a material composed of so-called antiparticles. It is believed that every particle we know of has an antimatter companion that is virtually identical to itself, but with the opposite charge. For example, an electron has a negative charge. But its antiparticle, called a positron, has the same mass but a positive charge. When a particle and its antiparticle meet, they annihilate each other – disappearing in a burst of light.

Such particles were first predicted by British physicist Paul Dirac when he was trying to combine the two great ideas of early modern physics: relativity and quantum mechanics. Previously, scientists were stumped by the fact that it seemed to predict that particles could have energies lower than when they were at "rest" (ie pretty much doing nothing). This seemed impossible at the time, as it meant that energies could be negative.

Dirac, however, accepted that the equations were telling him that particles are really filling a whole "sea" of these lower energies – a sea that had so far been invisible to physicists as they were only looking "above the surface". He envisioned that all of the "normal" energy levels that exist are accounted for by "normal" particles.

However, when a particle jumps up from a lower energy state, it appears as a normal particle but leaves a "hole", which appears to us as a strange, mirror-image particle – antimatter.

Despite initial scepticism, examples of these particle-antiparticle pairs were soon found. For example, they are produced when cosmic rays hit the Earth's atmosphere. There is even evidence that the energy in thunderstorms produces anti-electrons, called positrons. These are also produced in some radioactive decays, a process used in many hospitals in Positron Emission Tomography (PET) scanners, which allow precise imaging within human bodies. Nowadays, experiments at the Large Hadron Collider (LHC) can produce matter and antimatter, too.

Matter-antimatter mystery

Physics predicts that matter and antimatter must be created in almost equal quantities, and that this would have been the case during the Big Bang. What's more, it is predicted that the laws of physics should be the same if a particle is interchanged with its antiparticle – a relationship known as CP symmetry. However, the universe we see doesn't seem to obey these rules. It is almost entirely made of matter, so where did all the antimatter go? It is one of the biggest mysteries in physics to date.

Experimental area at CERN including the alpha experiment.
Mikkel D. Lund/wikimeda, CC BY-SA

Experiments have shown that some radioactive decay processes do not produce an equal amount of antiparticles and particles. But it is not enough to explain the disparity between amounts of matter and antimatter in the universe. Consequently, physicists such as myself at the LHC, on ATLAS, CMS and LHCb, and others doing experiments with neutrinos such as T2K in Japan, are looking for other processes that could explain the puzzle.

Other groups of physicists such as the Alpha Collaboration at CERN are working at much lower energies to see if the properties of antimatter really are the mirror of their matter partners. Their latest results show that an anti-hydrogen atom (made up of an anti-proton and an anti-electron, or positron) is electrically neutral to an accuracy of less than one billionth of the charge of an electron. Combined with other measurements, this implies that the positron is equal and opposite to the charge of the electron to better than one part in a billion – confirming what is expected of antimatter.

However, a great many mysteries remain. Experiments are also investigating whether gravity affects antimatter in the same way that it affects matter. If these exact symmetries are shown to be broken, it will require a fundamental revision of our ideas about physics, affecting not only particle physics but also our understanding of gravity and relativity.

In this way, antimatter experiments are allowing us to put our understanding of the fundamental workings of the universe to new and exciting tests. Who knows what we will find?

CHAPTER EIGHT

Way Of Science Alert

Antimatter is the general name given to a category of particles that share the same properties as other forms of matter, only with a reversed charge. For example, the antimatter particle called a positron shares all the properties of an electron, but with a positive charge instead of a negative one.

How was antimatter discovered?

The idea of an anti-particle was first developed by the physicist Paul Dirac in the late 1920s. Combining the emerging field of quantum mechanics with Albert Einstein's work on relativity, he revealed how particles behave at different speeds. Interpreting the consequences of his equations, Dirac suggested particles with the same mass and spin as electrons could theoretically exist, only with an opposite charge.

The following decade, tracks of particles left by cosmic rays inside a cloud chamber were considered to be the first sign that Dirac's anti-electrons existed in reality.

How does antimatter interact with normal matter?

When antimatter particles meet with their matter equivalents, each particle decays into gamma radiation.

This transformation of energy has made antimatter the perfect fuel for everything from engines to weapons in science fiction.

While it's a natural product of decay in radiating materials such as potassium, and can be generated using particle colliders, collecting enough in one place to serve as a source of power is challenging. For CERN to amass a gram of the material at its current rate of generation, it would take about 100 billion years.

Why is antimatter so rare?

So far there is nothing in physics that makes matter special. Both types of particle should exist in equal amounts, but why we don't see this remains one of the biggest mysteries in physics.

Since both forms of particles annihilate each other and leave only high energy radiation, it's also a mystery as to why we have particles of a particular variety at all.

CHAPTER NINE

Talk To How Stuff Works

How Antimatter Spacecraft Will Work

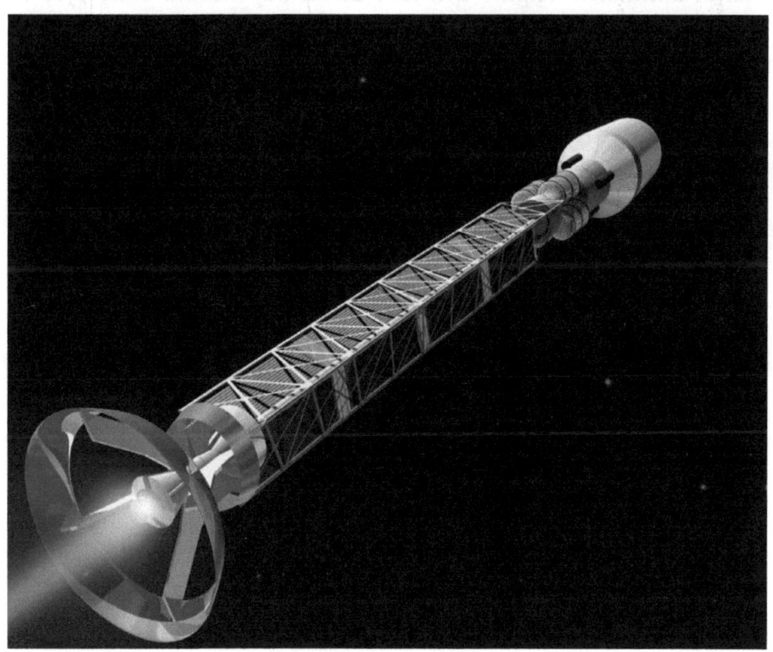

Antimatter spacecraft like this one could some day shorten a trip to Mars from 11 months to one month. Check out current spaceflight technology in these pictures of space shuttles. Photo courtesy NASA

"Engineering, stand by for warp drive." With that command, the "Star Trek" crew of the U.S.S. Enterprise prepared to hurl the spaceship through the cosmos at superluminal speeds. Warp drive is another one of those science fiction technologies, like teleportation and time travel, that have some scientific basis. It just hasn't been achieved yet. However, scientists are working on developing an interstellar spacecraft engine that is similar to the matter-antimatter engine of the Enterprise.

No engine is likely to generate superluminal speeds; the laws of physics prevent us from doing that, but we will be able to go many times faster than our current propulsion methods allow. A matter-antimatter engine will take us far beyond our solar system and let us reach nearby stars in a fraction of the time it would take a spacecraft propelled by a liquid-hydrogen engine, like the one used in the space shuttle. It's like the difference between driving an Indy race car and a 1971 Ford Pinto. In the Pinto, you'll eventually get to the finish line, but it will take 10 times longer than in the Indy car.

In this article, we will peer a few decades into the future of space travel to look at an antimatter spacecraft, and find out what antimatter actually is and how it will be used for an advanced propulsion system.

What is Antimatter?

In this composite image of the Crab Nebula, matter and antimatter are propelled nearly to the speed of light by the Crab pulsar. The images came from NASA's Chandra X-ray Observatory and the Hubble Space Telescope Photo by NASA/Getty Images

This isn't a trick question. Antimatter is exactly what you might think it is -- the opposite of normal matter, of which the majority of our universe is made. Until just recently, the presence of antimatter in our universe was considered to be only theoretical. In 1928, British physicist Paul A.M. Dirac revised Einstein's famous equation $E=mc^2$. Dirac said that Einstein didn't consider that the "m" in the equation -- mass -- could have negative properties as well as positive. Dirac's equation (E = + or - mc2) allowed for the existence of anti-particles in our universe. Scientists have since proven that several anti-particles exist.

These anti-particles are, literally, mirror images of normal matter. Each anti-particle has the same mass as its corresponding particle, but the electrical charges are reversed. Here are some antimatter discoveries of the 20th century:

- Positrons - Electrons with a positive instead of negative charge. Discovered by Carl Anderson in 1932, positrons were the first evidence that antimatter existed.
- Anti-protons - Protons that have a negative instead of the usual positive charge. In 1955, researchers at the Berkeley Bevatron produced an antiproton.
- Anti-atoms - Pairing together positrons and antiprotons, scientists at CERN, the European Organization for Nuclear Research, created the first anti-atom. Nine anti-hydrogen atoms were created, each lasting only 40 nanoseconds. As of 1998, CERN researchers were pushing the production of anti-hydrogen atoms to 2,000 per hour.

When antimatter comes into contact with normal matter, these equal but opposite particles collide to produce an explosion emitting pure radiation, which travels out of the point of the explosion at the speed of light. Both particles that created the explosion are completely annihilated, leaving behind other subatomic particles. The explosion that occurs when antimatter and matter interact transfers the entire mass of both objects into energy. Scientists believe that this energy is more powerful than any that can be generated by other propulsion methods.

So, why haven't we built a matter-antimatter reaction engine? The problem with developing antimatter propulsion is that there is a lack of antimatter existing in the universe. If there were equal amounts of matter and antimatter, we would likely see these reactions around us. Since antimatter doesn't exist around us, we don't see the light that would result from it colliding with matter.

It is possible that particles outnumbered anti-particles at the time of the Big Bang. As stated above, the collision of particles and anti-particles destroys both. And because there may have been more particles in the universe to start with, those are all that's left. There may be no naturally-existing anti-particles in our universe today. However, scientists discovered a possible deposit of antimatter near the center of the galaxy in 1977. If that does exist, it would mean that antimatter exists naturally, and the need to make our own antimatter would be eliminated.

For now, we will have to create our own antimatter. Luckily, there is technology available to create antimatter through the use of high-energy particle colliders, also called "atom smashers." Atom smashers, like CERN, are large tunnels lined with powerful supermagnets that circle around to propel atoms at near-light speeds. When an atom is sent through this accelerator, it slams into a target, creating particles. Some of these particles are antiparticles that are separated out by the magnetic field. These high-energy particle accelerators only produce one or two picograms of antiprotons each year. A picogram is a trillionth of a gram. All of the antiprotons produced at CERN in one year would be enough to light a 100-watt electric light bulb for three seconds. It will take tons of antiprotons to travel to interstellar destinations.

Matter-Antimatter Engine

Antimatter spacecraft like the one in this artist concept could carry us beyond the solar system at amazing speeds. Photo courtesy Laboratory for Energetic Particle Science at Penn State

University

NASA is possibly only a few decades away from developing an antimatter spacecraft that would cut fuel costs to a fraction of what they are today. In October 2000, NASA scientists announced early designs for an antimatter engine that could generate enormous thrust with only small amounts of antimatter fueling it. The amount of antimatter needed to supply the engine for a one-year trip to Mars could be as little as a millionth of a gram, according to a report in that month's issue of Journal of Propulsion and Power.

Matter-antimatter propulsion will be the most efficient propulsion ever developed, because 100 percent of the mass of the matter and antimatter is converted into energy. When matter and antimatter collide, the energy released by their annihilation releases about 10 billion times the energy that chemical energy such as hydrogen and oxygen combustion, the kind used by the space shuttle, releases. Matter-antimatter reactions are 1,000 times more powerful than the nuclear fission produced in nuclear power plants and 300 times more powerful than nuclear fusion energy. So, matter-antimatter engines have the potential to take us farther with less fuel. The problem is creating and storing the antimatter. There are three main components to a matter-antimatter engine:

Magnetic storage rings - Antimatter must be separated from normal matter so storage rings with magnetic fields can move the antimatter around the ring until it is needed to create energy.

Feed system - When the spacecraft needs more power, the antimatter will be released to collide with a target of matter, which releases energy.

Magnetic rocket nozzle thruster - Like a particle collider on Earth, a long magnetic nozzle will move the energy created by the matter-antimatter through a thruster.

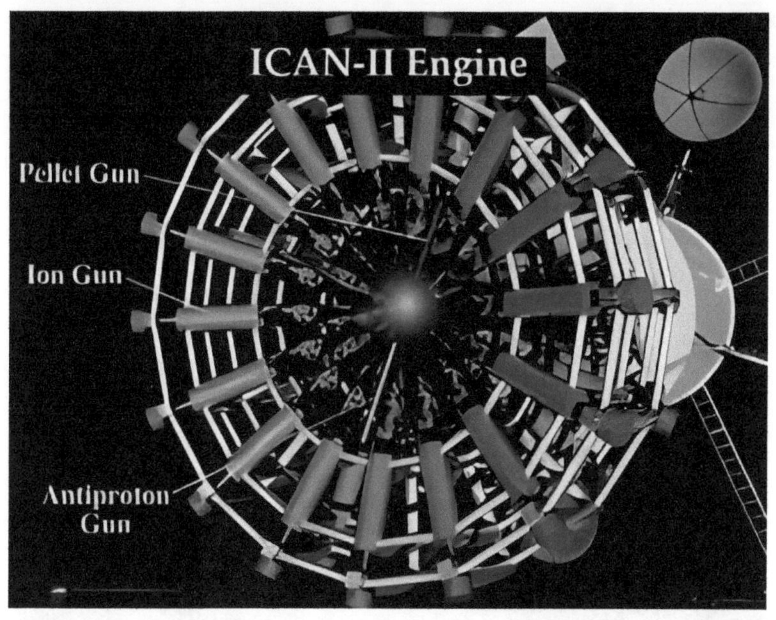

The storage rings on the spacecraft will hold the antimatter. Photo courtesy Laboratory for Energetic Particle Science at Penn State University

Approximately 10 grams of antiprotons would be enough fuel to send a manned spacecraft to Mars in one month. Today, it takes nearly a year for an unmanned spacecraft to reach Mars. In 1996, the Mars Global Surveyor took 11 months to arrive at Mars. Scientists believe that the speed of an matter-antimatter powered spacecraft would allow man to go where no man has gone before in space. It would be possible to make trips to Jupiter and even beyond the heliopause, the point at which the sun's radiation ends. But it will still be a long time before astronauts are asking their starship's helmsman to take them to warp speed.

CHAPTER TEN

By Space

The Mystery of Antimatter

One of the big questions lingering about our universe is why there is so much more matter than antimatter. (Image credit: GiroScience / Shutterstock.com)

At the beginning of time, just moments after the Big Bang, numerous particles came into existence; at the same time, an almost equal number of antiparticles appeared. These subatomic exotics are nearly identical to their ordinary particle kin, but differ in some key ways. When matter and antimatter meet, the two annihilate one another, which means that the dawn of the universe included a spectacular microscopic fireworks display.

Antimatter is sort of like a mirror to ordinary matter, having the same mass but an opposite charge. Neutrinos, which have no charge, are thought to be their own antiparticles, although experiments have yet to confirm this theory. Along with being created shortly after the Big Bang, antimatter can arise from a wide variety of nuclear processes, and can exist for a short time in any of the particle accelerators worldwide.

Since the beginning of time

Antimatter first came to researchers' attention in 1928, when British physicist Paul Dirac was looking at solutions to an equation that describes the movement of an electron traveling near the speed of light.

"Just as the equation x^2 = 4 can have two possible solutions (x = 2 or x = −2), so Dirac's equation could have two solutions, one for an electron with positive energy, and one for an electron with negative energy," according to the European Organization for Nuclear Research's (CERN) history of antimatter.

Dirac realized that the negatively-charged electron should have an opposing partner with a positive charge. These positive electrons, or positrons, were discovered a few years later by physicist Carl Anderson at the California Institute of Technology, who was studying highly energetic cosmic rays from space that strike the Earth's atmosphere, producing a shower of other particles. Anderson witnessed, in his particle detector, something with the same mass as an electron but with a positive charge.

Dirac was awarded the Nobel Prize in physics in 1933 for his discovery; Anderson's research won him the prize in 1936. In his acceptance speech, Dirac speculated that perhaps the Earth just happened to be composed of matter but that there could be stars made of antimatter lurking out in the universe.

But when astronomers train their telescopes out into space, they don't see antimatter stars nor any large pockets of antimatter anywhere in the cosmos. The reason for this lack and the fact that the universe seems to be comprised entirely of particles and not antiparticles, was called "one of the great mysteries in physics" in a 2012 paper in the New Journal of Physics.

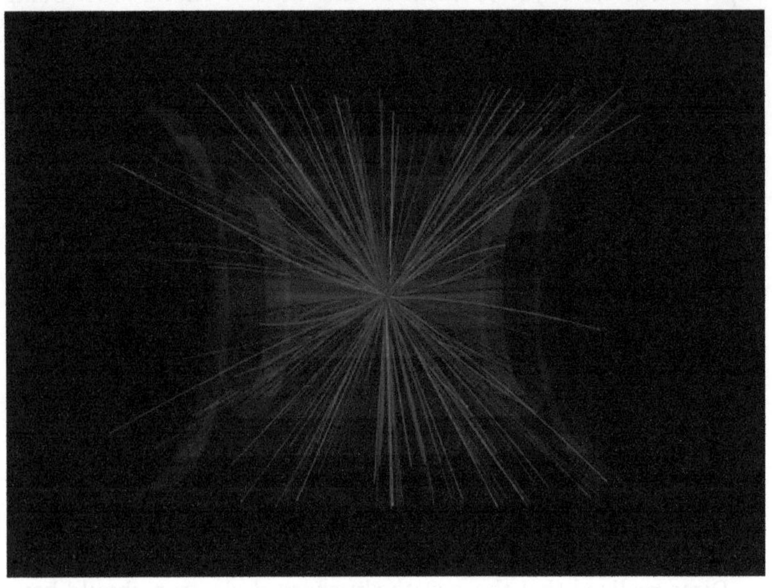

Researchers calculated the weight of an antiproton, a finding that could shed light on the puzzle over what happened to all the antimatter that was created in equal proportion to matter in the Big Bang. Here, tracks of particle collisions in CERN's Large Hadron Collider, create conditions just moments after the Big Bang. (Image credit: CERN)

A persistent mystery

In 2018, scientists were even more perplexed when they made the most precise measurement of antimatter to date and found that antimatter and matter behave nearly identically. The finding suggests that particles and their opposites should have been created in equal numbers at the beginning of the universe; however, if true, the fact that matter prevails over antimatter is ever more difficult to reconcile.

Researchers are diligently seeking the factor that explains the dominance of matter over antimatter in our cosmos. Calculations suggest that just after the Big Bang, when particles and antiparticles annihilated one another, there was a slight imbalance in their numbers. Less than one in every billion ordinary particles survived the melee and went on to form all the matter around us today. But why?

Scientists worldwide are working to determine if a neutrino acts as its own antiparticle, which would have allowed a small fraction of neutrinos to transition from antimatter to matter at the universe's inception. In this scenario, a slight matter imbalance would have existed back then.

Antimatter has been created and sustained in small quantities in particle-physics laboratories. Some research teams have gone so far as to create antiprotons, and drive them around in a van so that physicists at CERN could transport them to a nearby facility.

Readers of Dan Brown's book "Angels and Demons" (Pocket Books, 2000) — which (spoiler alert) involves a plot to blow up the Vatican using antimatter — might worry about such experiments. But worry not: If CERN scientists took all the antimatter they ever created and annihilated it with matter, they would barely have enough energy to light a single electric light bulb for a few minutes, according to a website FAQ from the CERN laboratory.

CHAPTER ELEVEN

Article of Astronomy

Where did the universe's antimatter go? Scientists inch closer to solving the mystery

New particle accelerator data from the T2K experiment could finally tell us where all the antimatter went.

The K in T2K refers to Kamioka, Japan, where the Super-Kamiokande Detector resides deep underground. The detector uses this giant, water-filled cylinder to detect neutrinos shot from 180 miles away in Tokai — the T in the project's name. Recent data show how neutrinos and antineutrinos change from one type to another — at different rates — as they travel.

In 1996, Discover reported on a new experiment that would probe the far universe for signs of antimatter. These particles are theoretically identical in behavior to the ones we know, but with opposing electrical charges, among other differences.

Physicists' theories about the Big Bang say there should have been equal amounts of matter and antimatter created during the event. But we live in a universe full of matter, with little antimatter in sight.

There are different explanations for this, including that all of the antimatter might just be too far away to see. The search for distant antistars and antigalaxies was the focus of our April 1996 article, "The Antimatter Mission," which chronicled the genesis of an experiment called the Alpha Magnetic Spectrometer (AMS). The experiment set out to measure cosmic rays to see if any of them came from antimatter.

The AMS has been running on the International Space Station since 2011, but it has yet to turn up much evidence for antigalaxies and the like. It could be that our universe is largely empty of antimatter, which poses another question: Where did it all go?

Scientists have long posited that slight differences in how matter and antimatter behave could have led matter to win out in the moments after the Big Bang. But finding those asymmetries has proved difficult. Now, physicists with Japan's T2K experiment have published data that move us closer to an answer.

The Alpha Magnetic Spectrometer has been collecting data from the International Space Station since 2011, but has yet to turn up evidence for antimatter.

T2K scientists are tracking a curious property of neutrinos, hard-to-detect particles that rarely interact with matter. Neutrinos change type, or flavor, as they travel — for example, muon neutrinos might turn into electron neutrinos.

The T2K experiment has been watching how both regular neutrinos and antineutrinos oscillate between flavors, and they've noticed there's a slight disparity in how they behave.

The transition of a muon neutrino to an electron neutrino happens at a higher rate than that of a muon antineutrino to an electron antineutrino, says Mark Hartz, a particle physicist at Canada's York University and co-author of a recent Nature paper on the T2K data. The data provide further evidence that there could be some slight asymmetries between normal matter and antimatter, perhaps enough to explain why the universe today is almost exclusively made of matter.

But Nobel laureate Samuel Ting, the principal investigator of the AMS experiment, says we need more data to truly say antimatter isn't out there somewhere.

"This neutrino experiment only says, 'From Earth, we observe in space more matter than antimatter,' " he says. "It does not say, 'Antimatter disappeared.' "

Ting's views may not represent the majority opinion among scientists, but the physicist is undaunted: "If you don't look, then really you will never know."

CHAPTER TWELVE

Idea of Science Focus

What is antimatter, and why is it missing from the Universe today?

Particles and antiparticles have opposite properties, such as electric charge. For instance, the antiparticle of the negative electron is the positive positron. Every physics process we know of creates equal amounts of matter and antimatter.

When a particle meets its antiparticle however, it 'annihilates', ultimately into high-energy photons. As such, the Universe should contain no matter or antimatter, and just be a sea of photons. Instead, it contains enough matter to make about two trillion galaxies and, as far as we can tell, no antimatter.

A clue to what happened to all the antimatter comes from the fact that the 'afterglow' of the Big Bang (the cosmic background radiation) contains about 10 billion photons for every particle of matter in today's Universe. This tells us that, in the Big Bang, there were 10 billion and one particles of matter for every 10 billion of antimatter, and after an orgy of annihilation there were 10 billion photons for every particle of matter.

Physicists have long been looking for a subtle asymmetry in the laws of physics that explains this excess of matter over antimatter in the Big Bang. And they think they may have found it in the behaviour of neutrinos.

Neutrinos are ghostly subatomic particles that rarely interact with matter. (Hold up your thumb; about 100 billion neutrinos, generated by nuclear reactions in the Sun, pass through your thumbnail every second.) Neutrinos come in three types and each neutrino continually changes from an electron-neutrino to a muon-neutrino to a tau-neutrino and back again.

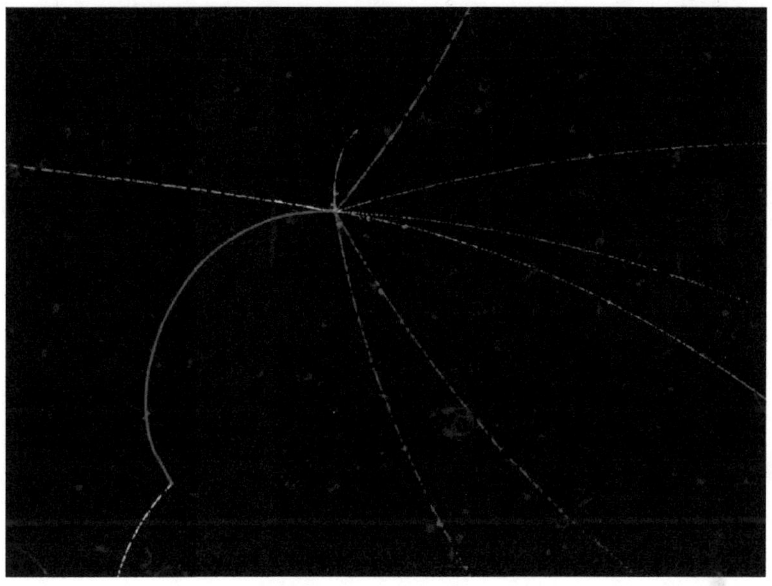

Positive particles (red) and negative particles (green) curve away from the moment of annihilation in this false-colour bubble chamber image

Since 2016, physicists at the T2K experiment in Japan have been trying to show that neutrinos behave differently to antineutrinos. To do this, they generate beams of muon-neutrinos and muon-antineutrinos at a facility in Tokai and send them to the giant underground Super-Kamiokande detector, 295km away.

So far, they've detected more electron-neutrinos and fewer electron-antineutrinos than expected, suggesting neutrinos do behave differently to antineutrinos. It's a small effect that needs to be confirmed, but it could provide the mechanism for creating a matter-dominated Universe.

Neutrinos have too little mass to have made much difference to the Universe. Crucially, however, they only spin clockwise around their direction of flight, and physicists wonder whether neutrinos and antineutrinos had super-heavy partners with opposite spin in the Big Bang.

These ultra-heavy particles would have been able to form only in the high-energy conditions of the Big Bang and would have quickly decayed into the particles we see today. In doing so, they could have imprinted their asymmetry on the cosmos, producing the 10 billion and one particles of matter for every 10 billion of antimatter needed to explain why we live in a Universe exclusively of matter.

CHAPTER THIRTEEN

Information Of India Today

Where is all the antimatter? Even creating antihydrogen in a lab cannot explain its lack in the universe

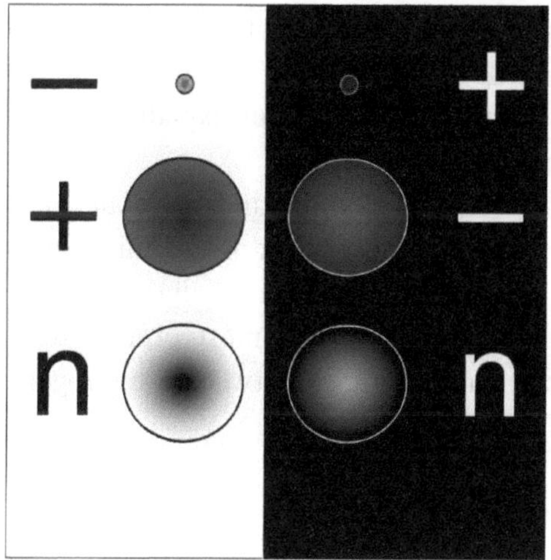

If matter and antimatter were created together in the Big Bang, where is all the antimatter now? Scientists have created an antihydrogen atom a\nd are trying to find answers to this question.

All that exists around us, everything we can see or touch, is matter. It could be as small as an electron to as large as the sun around which our Earth revolves. All of it is matter, and as per our knowledge of science, every particle of matter has an equal measure of antimatter. But where is all the antimatter in the universe?

Physicists at CERN, the massive underground particle research lab in Europe, revealed on Wednesday that they have created an antimatter particle in the lab as a part of the ALPHA experiment. The scientists have created an atom of 'antihydrogen' and have been observing it in order to solve one of the biggest mysteries of science.

The hydrogen is the simplest form of matter. It consists of just one electron revolving around one proton.

What is the main target of the CERN experiment?

The main target of the scientists is to discover whether matter and antimatter particle behave in the same way. Noting even a tiny difference in behavior might help us explain the lack of antimatter particles in the universe.

It would also turn over the Standard Model of physics which tells us matter is the building block of the universe and explains its behavior, but offers no explanation for all the missing antimatter.

However, till now, even the "most precise test to date" was unable to locate any difference between a hydrogen atom and the antihydrogen atom.

What do we know about matter and antimatter?

It is believed in science that when the Big Bang took place, it created equal masses of matter and antimatter with opposite electric charges. When matter and antimatter particles come into contact, they annihilate each other leaving behind a massive amount of energy.

In the Star Trek series, this is the power source for the spacecraft.

Is there really no antimatter in the universe?

According to physicists, shortly after the Big Bang, matter and antimatter did meet and annihilate each other. But that would mean that today's universe shouldn't consist of anything apart from pure leftover energy.

Moreover, scientists also say that matter comprises just 4.9 per cent of the universe, while dark matter (the mysterious substance that makes space look dark and can only be felt by their gravitational pull on other objects) takes up 26.8 per cent, and dark energy makes for the remaining 68.3 per cent.

From human observation, it can be said that antimatter doesn't really exist except for when it is created by specialized places like the CERN and that too for a temporary period, or when it is rarely produced in some high-energy instances like cosmic rays.

Nevertheless, the universe is too large to imagine and only a tiny fraction of it has been observed, even by the most powerful telescopes on the planet.

Some scientists believe that the "missing" antimatter does exist and it forms antigalaxies made from antistars and antiplanets which we have not observed yet.

How the research team created and studied the antihydrogen atom

Mirrored hydrogen particles were created by the CERN team by using positrons left from high-energy particle collisions by CERN and binding the to the twins of electrons called positrons.

Antihydrogen atoms were created as a result and were held in a magnetic trap so that they don't come into contact with matter and self-annihilate.

Atoms of different types of matter absorb different frequencies of light and so, to understand more about the antihydrogen atoms, their reaction to laser light was then studied. It was seen that both hydrogen and antihydrogen atoms reacted in the same way.

The team is trying to progress with the experiment and fine tune it to better understand the possible differences that could emerge.

"Although the precision still falls short for that of ordinary hydrogen, the rapid progress made by ALPHA suggests hydrogen-like precision in antihydrogen (measurements) are now within reach," said Jeffrey Hangst from the ALPHA experiment team, as per the CERN press release.

CHAPTER FOURTEEN

Final Mystery of Antimatter

The Mystery of Antimatter

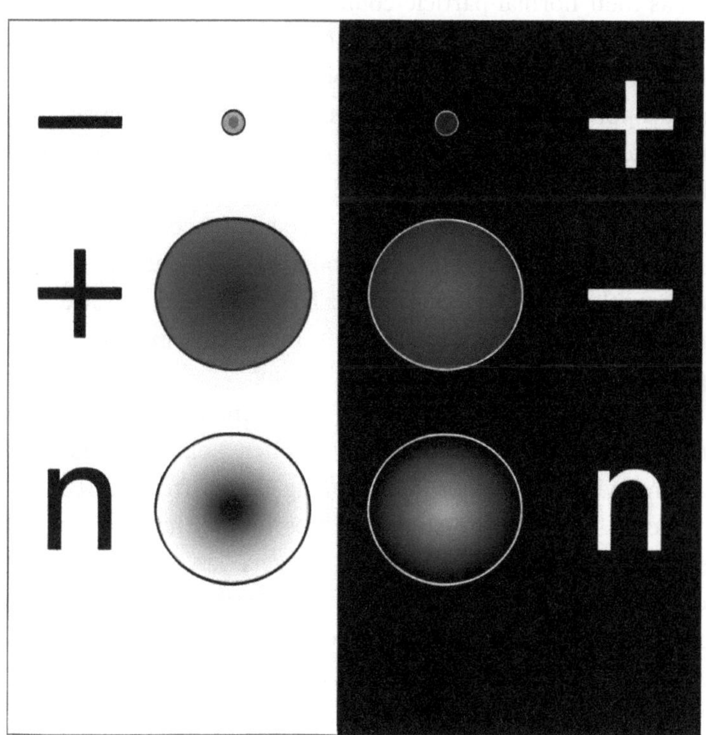

Particles and Antiparticles (credit: Anybody, cc by-sa 3.0)

Despite being prevalent in science fiction stories for generation, antimatter is real, and rooted firmly in modern scientific theory. Its existence was confirmed in 1955 by scientists at the University of California, Berkeley, for which they were awarded the Nobel prize in physics just four years later. When exposed to regular matter, antimatter annihilates, releasing energy that can in principle be harnessed to do work–power a lightbulb, or a city. While potential applications for harnessing such energy abound, none have ever fully materialized. The reasons why reveal one of the largest unsolved problems in physics today.

Antimatter refers to particles very similar to the ordinary matter with which we are all familiar. Such anti-particles have the same mass as their normal-particle counterparts, but are their opposites in some respects. For example, an anti-electron, commonly called a positron, has the same mass as a normal electron but has a positive charge opposite to that of the electron's normal electric charge. Antimatter is routinely produced in particle accelerators and in collision of high-energy particles in the earth's atmosphere. The mystery of antimatter lies in its marked absence. As best we can tell, the universe around us is composed almost entirely of regular matter, with no antimatter in sight. To understand why we should expect to find antimatter at all, it helps to think back to the beginning of the universe and the big bang.

The Big Bang Theory was developed in the early part of the 20th century to explain observations by Slipher, Lemaitre, and Hubble that the visible galaxies are moving away from earth in all directions. Two interpretations are possible: Either the earth is at the center of a cosmic explosion of galaxies, or space itself is everywhere expanding. The latter explanation is of course much more tenable, and has been the consensus view ever since. The effect is like that of blowing up a balloon or stretching a rubber band. Two marks on the surface of the rubber will move apart, not because of relative motion of the dots along the rubber, but because the space in which they exist is stretching apart.

Naturally, upon observing the continual expansion of space, one is forced to imagine what things looked like a million or a billion years ago. Things then must have been much closer together, more dense, and hotter. In fact, it's relatively simple to figure out when everything must have been at one point ... a little over 13.8 billion years ago by modern estimates. Around that time, as the theory goes, all of space and matter (and time) exploded out from that point, cooling as it expanded. Quantum fluctuations of photons in this plasma continually created pairs of particles, electrons and positrons, particles and antiparticles. These particles were created, and annihilated almost immediately. As the plasma continued to expand and cool, some of the particles and antiparticles were created but did not annihilate, and the particles eventually agglomerated to form the atoms, stars, planets, and everything we see around us today.

But what of the anti-particles? Where did they go? We know the processes that created all the matter we see, and we know that an equal amount of antimatter must have been simultaneously created. But where is it? This is one of the largest unanswered questions in modern cosmology, and many scientists are hard at work trying to solve the puzzle. One of them is Hui Chen, who lead a team at Lawrence Livermore in 2008 to produce more antimatter than had ever before been produced in a lab. She and her team used high-energy lasers to illuminate gold targets, many times thicker than previous targets. The laser photons ionize the gold atoms, creating high-energy electrons which traverse the gold target, losing energy as they go. Some of this energy transforms (via Einstein's famous mass-energy equality) into positrons and electrons. Optimization of the process allowed Chen and her team to create far more antimatter particles than ever before, opening up the possibility of new research into the enigmatic asymmetry of matter and antimatter in the universe.

Will we find other planets, solar systems, and galaxies made of antimatter? NASA is betting we just might. If so, it would rank as one of the amazing discoveries of mankind. If not, then perhaps there is new physics awaiting us that we don't yet understand, and that would be an equally exciting discovery.

CHAPTER FIFTEEN

Where is "The Missing Antimatter"

what is antimatter

To understand what antimatter is, you need to know what matter is and what existed before matter and antimatter in the universe?

so come i am going to start i will tell you in brief if you want to read it in detail then you can read my blog which i have posted earlier on this website "the real shape of universe" so what is it Let's understand antimatter-

At starts of universe, the vector field of universe was '0'

Vector field- As fields exist in universal field theory and in the beginning there was a universal field and all the fields have been. generated from that.

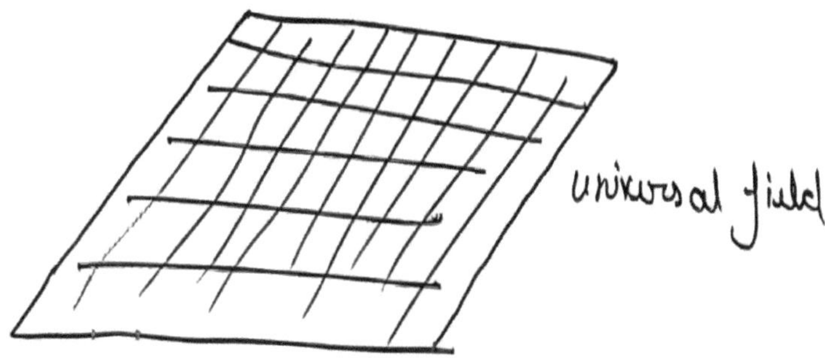

Universal field

The meaning of the vector field of universe is that the universe field was at the beginning of the universe but was not constant and does not fix the same amplitude up and down in the sides of its normal axis then its vector field is not zero.

Upper field distance – The perpendicular distance between the normal midpoint and upper field line is called upper field distance.

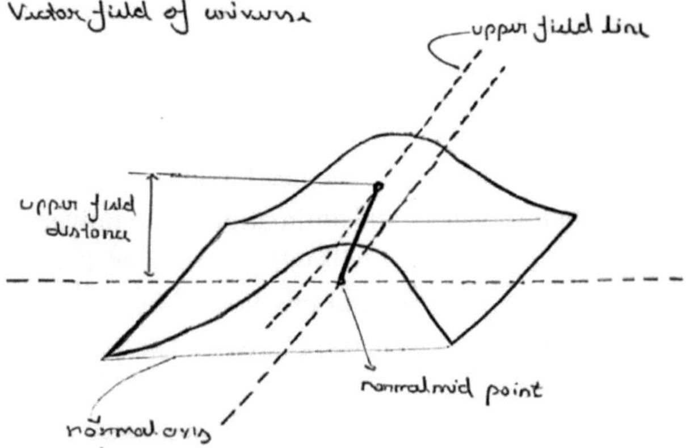

Upper field distance

Down field distance – The perpendicular distance between the normal midpoint and the down field line is called down field distance.

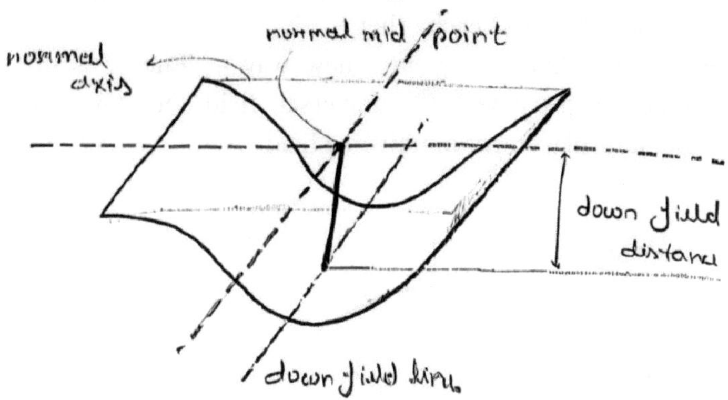

Down field distance

Normal midpoint(Nm)

- Upper field distance(U_d)

Down field distance (D_d)

Vector field (V_f)

Vector field of universe = Upper field distance - Down field distance

$V_f = U_d - D_d$

Upper field interaction point and Down field interaction point-

The point at which the perpendicular from the normal mid point intersects the upper field is called the upper field interaction point and similarly the point where the normal mid point intersects the Down field is called the Down field interaction point.

Upper field interaction point (Ui)

Down field interaction point(Di)

Hence the universal field that Ud and Dd are same, hence its vector field (Vf) is also zero.

Let us understand another great question, how energy and mass are the counterparts of each other –

So let us define energy in a new way – “Energy is the non permanent displacement of universal field”and “mass is the permanent displacement of universe field”

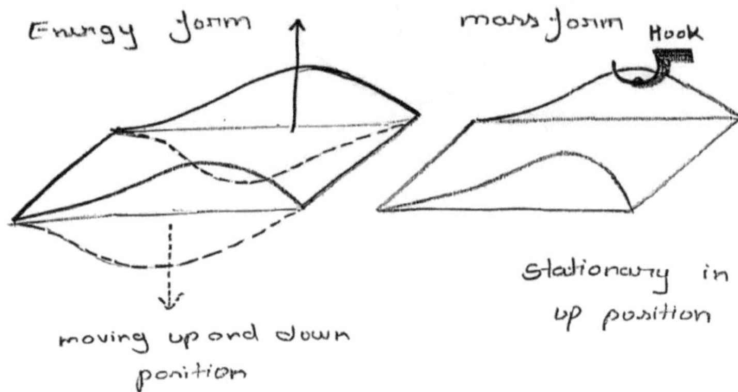

When some hook grabs the field, the field is unable to move,this is what we call energy to mass formation –

Here hook is not talking about any physical hook and there are such rules of physics which stop the field and do not allow it to move.

in upcoming topic i am going to describe what is that rule of physics what make the visible mass from energy.i believed that this concept change your learning direction of physics and will shock you.

how positive energy convert into matter

as i have discussed in detail that what is matter and what is antimatter and what is positive energy and negative energy .

come understand this in short term-

Universe is a such type of many of flat sheets that called according to me universal field and this universal field is moving in up and down position so it's displaced will be 0.

when it goes it up direction it called positive energy and when it goes in below direction then it calls negative energy now "some thing" Happened and that universal field stops in one direction then it converts in mass form and if that field stops in upper direction then we called it positive mass and if that field stops in below direction then it called antimatter.

Now your question will be that what is that "something" That stops universal field in one direction.

then come i am going to describe that hook which stops universal field in upper direction and construct matter.

Here hook is not talking about any physical hook and there are such rules of physics which stop the field and do not allow it to move.

Let us discuss such a hook –

Just as if we throw stones in a pond, the waves rise from the place of falling of the stone and move at some speed till the end, in the same way the curvature of energy and mass made in the universal field move.

Let us raise another basic question, as we know that the speed of light is the highest speed in the universe. We also know that no one can cross the speed of light.

It is obvious that we cannot cross the speed of light, but we can try to do it, have you ever thought so! That thing is different that we will not be able to cross the speed of light.

For example, if we try to push the thick wall of a fort by pushing it, will we be able to move it? no | But if we tried, then due to the action and that effort, some change must have come about the microscopic level inside the wall.

Similarly, we will also see this as we are talking about graviton. So in the case of graviton, the maximum speed of the mass form of a string can try to go three times the light speed, we will do the proof and detail of this in our other research paper "Creation of visible mass",now you just analyze it. Consider the data

Suppose a string of graviton tries to travel three times the speed of light, what will happen?

Here we are using Sir.A.Einstein's formula

$$m^* = \frac{m_o}{\sqrt{1-\frac{v^2}{c^2}}}$$

Here m^* = relative mass

V = velocity of object

C = speed of light

m_o = real mass of object

Let v = 3c

$$m^* = \frac{m_o}{\sqrt{1-\frac{(3c)^2}{c^2}}}$$

$$m^* = \frac{m_o}{\sqrt{1-\frac{9c^2}{c^2}}}$$

$$m^* = \frac{m_o}{\sqrt{-\frac{8c^2}{c^2}}}$$

here i = iota

$i = \sqrt{-1}$

$$m^* = \frac{m_0}{i\sqrt{8}}$$

Here we are seeing that what was our real mass is getting converted into Imaginary mass if we are trying to go beyond the speed of light – but it is not possible that the mass becomes negative so whatever happens The mass will always be POSITIVE, so as soon as we try to cross the speed of light, the value of (1- 〖v ^(2)/ 〖c

^(2)) must be minimum i (iyota).

Then –

$$\sqrt{1-\frac{v^2}{c^2}} = i^3$$

Both *of two side square*

$$[\sqrt{1-\frac{v^2}{c^2}}]^2 = i^6$$

$$1-\frac{v^2}{c^2} = -1$$

$$\frac{v^2}{c^2} = 2$$

$$v^2 = 2c^2$$

Here we people are getting an important result that as soon as we try to cross 1.414

times of speed of light, the same energy will be converted into mass i.e. will act like a hook which will work in the energy field. Can stop the momentum in the upper direction.

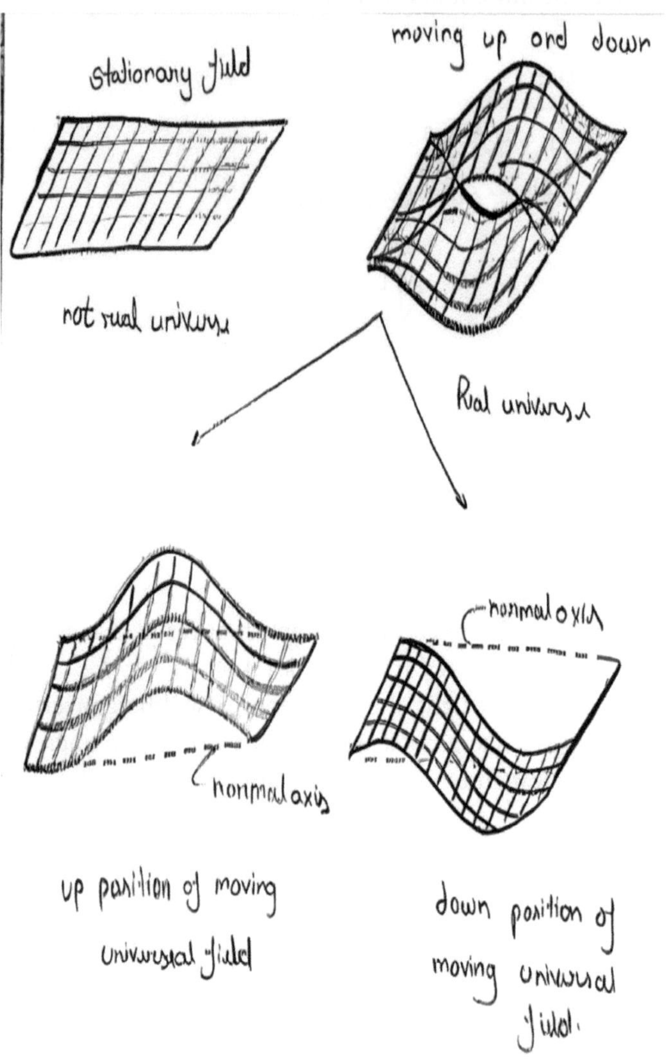

So i discussed in this topic how matter construct from positive energy in next topic i will discuss how antimatter change from negative energy.

how negative energy convert into antimatter

as i have discussed in detail that what is matter and what is antimatter and what is positive energy and negative energy .

come understand this in short term-

Universe is a such type of many of flat sheets that called according to me universal field and this universal field is moving in up and down position so it's displaced will be 0.

when it goes it up direction it called positive energy and when it goes in below direction then it calls negative energy now "some thing" Happened and that universal field stops in one direction then it converts in mass form and if that field stops in upper direction then we called it positive mass and if that field stops in below direction then it called antimatter.

Now your question will be that what is that "something" That stops universal field in one direction.

then come i am going to describe that hook which stops universal field in upper direction and construct matter.

Here hook is not talking about any physical hook and there are such rules of physics which stop the field and do not allow it to move.

Let us discuss such a hook –

Just as if we throw stones in a pond, the waves rise from the place of falling of the stone and move at some speed till the end, in the same way the curvature of energy and mass made in the universal field move.

Let us raise another basic question, as we know that the speed of light is the highest speed in the universe. We also know that no one can cross the speed of light.

It is obvious that we cannot cross the speed of light, but we can try to do it, have you ever thought so! That thing is different that we will not be able to cross the speed of light.

For example, if we try to push the thick wall of a fort by pushing it, will we be able to move it? no | But if we tried, then due to the action and that effort, some change must have come about the microscopic level inside the wall.

Similarly, we will also see this as we are talking about graviton. So in the case of graviton, the maximum speed of the mass form of a string can try to go three times the light speed, we will do the proof and detail of this in our other research paper "Creation of visible mass",now you just analyze it. Consider the data

Suppose a string of graviton tries to travel three times the speed of light, what will happen?

Here we are using Sir.A.Einstein's formula

$$m^* = \frac{m_\circ}{\sqrt{1-\frac{v^2}{c^2}}}$$

Here m^* = relative mass

V = velocity of object

C = speed of light

$m_\circ$ = real mass of object

Let v = 3c

$$m^* = \frac{m_\circ}{\sqrt{1-\frac{(3c)^2}{c^2}}}$$

$$m^* = \frac{m_\circ}{\sqrt{1-\frac{9c^2}{c^2}}}$$

$$m^* = \frac{m_\circ}{\sqrt{-\frac{8c^2}{c^2}}}$$

here i = iota

i= $\sqrt{-1}$

$$m^* = \frac{m_0}{i\sqrt{8}}$$

As we took (1- 〖v ^(2)/ 〖c ^(2)) = i ^(3) for positive mass so that i ^(3) and i multiplied by Make i ^(4) and get the relative mass positive, in the same way we are keeping (1- 〖 v ^(2)/ 〖 c ^(2)) = i ^(2) for antimatter So that i ^(2) and i multiply to make i ^(3) and i ^(2) gives us -1 and one "i" remain so that it shows the property of antimatter.

Then –

$$\sqrt{1-\frac{v^2}{c^2}} = i^3$$

Both *of two side square*

$$[\sqrt{1-\frac{v^2}{c^2}}]^2 = i^6$$

$$1-\frac{v^2}{c^2} = -1$$

$$\frac{v^2}{c^2} = 2$$

$$v^2 = 2c^2$$

Hence the conclusion is that if the velocity of the energy curvature in the universal field becomes zero, then a hook will be provided to the negative energy which will create antimatter.

here we have seen how antimatter takes form from negative energy and in next topic i will discuss where is missing antimatter.

where is missing antimatter

if you have not read my last two topics first "how matter creates from positive energy" and second "how antimatter creates from negative energy" then there i told that how matter and antimatter take their form and also describe what what is the conditions for constructing matter and anti matter so if you do not read them then please read them then you will be able to understand this topic "where is missing antimatter.

so to understand where is missing antimatter you have to know how antimatter creates i have described it in detail in last topic here i am describing only in brief.

as we have taken=i^3 for matter so that i^3 and i can give i^4 after multiply and relative mass can convert into positive mass similarly we are taking

= i ^2 for antimatter

so that i ^2 and i can give us i^3 after multiply and i^2 can give us -1 and one "i" remain so that it can show the property of antimatter.

Then –

$$\sqrt{1-\frac{v^2}{c^2}} = i^3$$

Both *of two side square*

$$[\sqrt{1-\frac{v^2}{c^2}}]^2 = i^6$$

$$1-\frac{v^2}{c^2} = -1$$

$$\frac{v^2}{c^2} = 2$$

$$v^2 = 2c^2$$

Hence the conclusion is that if the velocity of the energy curvature in the universe field becomes zero, then a hook will be provided to the negative energy which will create antimatter.

But it will happen in very rear case that the velocity of energy curvature becomes zero.

This is possible only when the energy curvature of the same energy limit collides with each other from the opposite direction and reduces each other's velocity to zero.

There is very little chance that this can happen, so therefore we get to see less antimatter in the universe than expected.

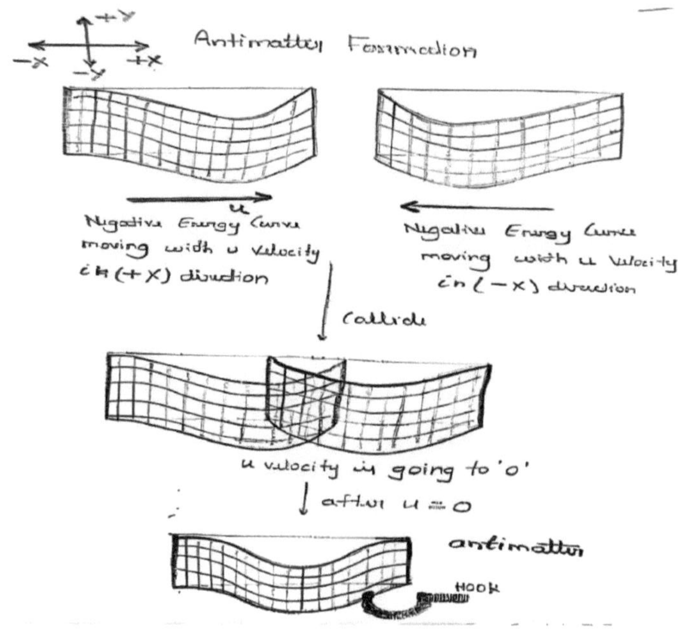

Antimatter Formation

so get a such type of condition is very difficult work for nature so we get there is missing antimatter but the negative energy is equal to positive energy and most of positive energy is converting i matter but negative energy is not converting in to antimatter.

Printed by Libri Plureos GmbH in Hamburg,
Germany